Teachers, librarians, and kids from
across Canada are talking about the
Canadian Flyer Adventures.
Here's what some of them had to say:

Great Canadian historical content, excellent illustrations,
and superb closing historical facts (I love the kids'
commentary!). ~ *SARA S., TEACHER, ONTARIO*

As a teacher–librarian I welcome this series with open
arms. It fills the gap for Canadian historical adventures
at an early reading level! There's fast action, interesting,
believable characters, and great historical information.
~ *MARGARET L., TEACHER–LIBRARIAN, BRITISH COLUMBIA*

The *Canadian Flyer Adventures* will transport young
readers to different eras of our past with their appealing
topics. Thank goodness there are more artifacts in that old
dresser ... they are sure to lead to even more escapades.
~ *SALLY B., TEACHER–LIBRARIAN, MANITOBA*

When I shared the book with a grade 1–2 teacher at
my school, she enjoyed the book, noting that her students
would find it appealing because of the action-adventure
and short chapters. ~ *HEATHER J., TEACHER AND
LIBRARIAN, NOVA SCOTIA*

Newly independent readers will fly through
each *Canadian Flyer Adventure,* and be asking for
the next installment! Children will enjoy the fast-paced
narrative, the personalities of the main characters, and
the drama of the dangerous situations the children
find themselves in. ~ *PAM L., LIBRARIAN, ONTARIO*

I love the fact that these are Canadian adventures—kids should know how exciting Canadian history is. Emily and Matt are regular kids, full of curiosity, and I can see readers relating to them. ~ *JEAN K., TEACHER, ONTARIO*

What kids told us:

I would like to have the chance to ride on a magical sled and have adventures. ~ *EMMANUEL*

I would like to tell the author that her book is amazing, incredible, awesome, and a million times better than any book I've read. ~ *MARIA*

I would recommend the *Canadian Flyer Adventures* series to other kids so they could learn about Canada too. The book is just the right length and hard to put down. ~ *PAUL*

The books I usually read are the full-of-fact encyclopedias. This book is full of interesting ideas that simply grab me. ~ *ELEANOR*

At the end of the book Matt and Emily say they are going on another adventure. I'm very interested in where they are going next! ~ *ALEX*

I like when Emily and Matt fly into the sky on a sled towards a new adventure. I can't wait for the next book! ~ *JI SANG*

Lost in the Snow

Frieda Wishinsky

Illustrated by Leanne Franson

MAPLE
TREE
PRESS

Maple Tree Press Books are published by Owlkids Books Inc.
10 Lower Spadina Avenue, Suite 400, Toronto, Ontario M5V 2Z2
www.mapletreepress.com

Text © 2008 Frieda Wishinsky   Illustrations © 2008 Leanne Franson

Distributed in Canada by Raincoast Books
9050 Shaughnessy Street, Vancouver, British Columbia V6P 6E5

Distributed in the United States by Publishers Group West
1700 Fourth Street, Berkeley, California 94710

Dedication
For my cousin, friend, and fellow writer, Jean-Luc Bouille

Acknowledgements
Many thanks to the hard-working Maple Tree team for their insightful comments
and steadfast support. Special thanks to Leanne Franson and Claudia Dávila for
their engaging and energetic illustrations and design.

Cataloguing in Publication Data
Wishinsky, Frieda
Lost in the snow / Frieda Wishinsky ; illustrated by Leanne Franson.

(Canadian flyer adventures ; 10)
ISBN 978-1-897349-40-3 (bound).   ISBN 978-1-897349-41-0 (pbk.)

1. Filles du roi—Juvenile fiction. 2. Canada—History—1663–1713 (New France)—
Juvenile fiction. I. Franson, Leanne II. Title. III. Series: Wishinsky, Frieda.
Canadian flyer adventures ; 10.

PS8595.I834L68 2008   jC813'.54   C2008-902039-1

Library of Congress Control Number: 2008925710

Design & art direction: Claudia Dávila
Illustrations: Leanne Franson

We acknowledge the financial support of the Canada Council   ONTARIO ARTS COUNCIL
for the Arts, the Ontario Arts Council, the Government   CONSEIL DES ARTS DE L'ONTARIO
of Canada through the Book Publishing Industry Development Program (BPIDP), and the
Government of Ontario through the Ontario Media Development Corporation's Book Initiative for
our publishing activities.

CONTENTS

HOW IT ALL BEGAN

Emily and Matt couldn't believe their luck. They discovered an old dresser full of strange objects in the tower of Emily's house. They also found a note from Emily's Great-Aunt Miranda: "The sled is yours. Fly it to wonderful adventures."

They found a sled right behind the dresser! When they sat on it, shimmery gold words appeared:

Rub the leaf
Three times fast.
Soon you'll fly
To the past.

The sled rose over Emily's house. It flew over their town of Glenwood. It sailed out of a cloud and into the past. Their adventures on the flying sled had begun! Where will the sled take them next? Turn the page to find out.

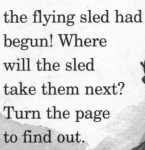

Quebec, New France
1665

1

Show Off

Matt took one look at Emily's face and knew something was wrong. "What's the matter?" he asked, bounding up her front porch stairs. He sat beside her on the top step.

"You know Sarah in my class?" asked Emily.

Matt nodded.

"Well, today she told everyone that her great, great, great, great-grandmother Therese was a king's daughter who came to Quebec from France in 1665 to get married. Sarah said that made *her* a princess, too. Then everyone wanted to hang out with Sarah at recess, even my friends Kari and Hannah. And no one spent time with me."

"Maybe it's not true. Maybe Sarah made the story up," said Matt.

"If she did, how can I prove it?"

"I saw an embroidered handkerchief in the dresser in your tower. It was beside the railroad whistle that took us on our last sled adventure. The label said, "Quebec, New France, 1664—or maybe 1665.""

Emily's eyes widened. "You did? That's terrific! Come on! We *have* to go there today. Let's check the tower room right now."

"But what if you find out that Sarah told the truth? What if Therese really was the king's daughter?" asked Matt, following Emily up the rickety stairs to the tower room.

"No way," said Emily, pushing the door open. "There couldn't be any king's daughters in Canada. They wouldn't want to leave their big fancy palaces in France. They wouldn't want to wear pioneer clothes instead of gorgeous gowns, or eat rabbit stew instead of sipping tea at parties with their ladies-in-waiting."

"There's only one way to find out," said Matt, opening the third drawer in the dresser. "And there's the handkerchief. Just as I remembered."

Emily picked it up. "It's so delicate and pretty. And the label *does* say, Quebec, New France, 1665. I can't wait to prove that show-off Sarah is wrong!"

Matt pulled the sled from behind the dresser. "I have my digital recorder. Do you have your sketchbook?"

"Yes," said Emily. "Look!"

Shimmery gold words were forming at the front of the sled beside the maple leaf.

Rub the leaf
Three times fast.
Soon you'll fly
To the past.

Emily and Matt hopped on the sled. Emily rubbed the maple leaf. Immediately, thick fog enveloped the sled. When the fog lifted, they were flying. They flew over Emily's house, over their town of Glenwood, and into the fluffy white cloud.

When the sled burst out of the cloud, they peered down.

"We're heading for a farm!" said Emily. "There's smoke coming out of the chimney. I bet someone's cooking. I hope they're not making rabbit stew! I could never eat a bunny!"

2

Go Back

The sled crunched down on a pile of autumn leaves beside some trees.

Emily and Matt slid off. They looked at their clothes. Matt was wearing a tuque, a white shirt with a wide collar, a dark jacket, a red wool scarf, leggings, a sash for a belt, and clog-like boots.

Emily wore a bonnet, a long blue and yellow dress under a shawl, and wooden shoes, too.

"Let's hide the sled in a pile of leaves in the woods," suggested Matt.

They dragged the sled through a clearing into the woods. After covering it with leaves, they headed for the farmhouse.

As they neared the house, a young woman in a long brown dress and a white apron ran outside. She looked about eighteen. She sank down on a log, put her head in her hands, and sobbed.

Emily and Matt hurried over to her.

"Are you okay?" asked Emily in French.

Emily glanced at Matt as she spoke. She was speaking French! She'd only taken a little French in school. The magic was amazing.

The young woman looked up. Her green eyes were red and puffy. She wiped her tears away with an embroidered handkerchief.

"I'm fine," she muttered.

"But you were crying," said Matt. He was speaking French, too!

"It's just..." mumbled the young woman. Then she burst into tears once more. She wiped them away again and took a deep breath. "I am sorry. I did not mean to cry in front of anyone. It is just that I am a king's daughter and now everything has changed. My name is Claire Dubois."

Emily gasped. "You're a king's daughter?"

"But of course. Surely you have heard that King Louis XIV has sent hundreds of young French women to Quebec to marry settlers."

"Hundreds?" said Matt.

"Maybe more," said Claire.

Emily and Matt stared at each other. How was that possible?

"The king has hundreds of daughters?" Emily blurted out.

"No," said Claire. "We are not really his daughters. It is just a name he has given to the group of women who have come here at the king's request."

"So you are *not* a princess?" said Emily, winking at Matt.

Claire smiled for the first time since they met her. "I am not a princess. I am just a poor farm girl. And now I am an unwanted stepmother."

Just then, a girl of Matt and Emily's age raced out of the farmhouse. She was wearing an outfit similar to Emily's.

She passed Claire without a word. Then she spun around and stuck her tongue out at her.

3

Ouch!

Claire turned white. She took a deep breath and stood up. "I must go to the bake-oven. My bread will be ready by now," she said, heading to the other end of the house.

"Who are you?" the girl asked Emily and Matt after Claire had left.

"I'm Emily, and this is Matt. We're visiting."

"My name's Marie Dubois. There are so many new people since the king's daughters came to New France."

"Is Claire your new mother?" asked Matt.

"She is *not* my mother, no matter what my father says. My real mother died. I do not want another mother."

"Claire seems nice," said Emily.

Marie wrinkled her nose like there was a bad smell in the air. "I wish she had never come. Why did my father have to marry again? So what if Marie is a good cook and helps take care of our house? Father and I were doing fine without *her*."

"Oh," said Emily.

"But that has nothing to do with you. I am glad to see you both. There are not many children living close by."

The anger in Marie's eyes disappeared. She was smiling now. "Come," she added, grabbing Emily's hand. "I will show you and Matt my animals. You will love Rosie."

"Who's Rosie?" asked Emily as she followed Marie down a pebbly path.

"You'll see!" sang Marie. She led them to a crooked wooden barn.

Marie pushed the door open. "Good morning, Rosie!" she called to a black-and-white cow. "These are my new friends, Emily and Matt. They have come to meet you."

Rosie swished her tail back and forth as Marie patted her head.

"Who would like to milk her?" Marie asked.

"I...I've never milked a cow," said Emily.

"It is easy," said Marie. "I will show you."

Marie sat on a small wooden stool beside Rosie. She put a wooden bucket under Rosie's udder. Then she grabbed a teat and pinched it. Milk spurted out into the bucket. She made it look easy.

"Now you!" said Marie to Emily. "And then you, Matt."

Emily took a deep breath. "Okay, I'll try." She patted Rosie on the head. "Good, Rosie," she said. Then Emily sat down on the little wooden stool. But before she could do anything, Rosie swatted Emily with her long tail.

"Ouch!" groaned Emily.

"Rosie!" said Marie. "Emily is our guest. That is not a nice way to treat guests."

"Why don't I try milking her another time?" asked Emily, rubbing her sore head.

Marie nodded. "I will finish milking her now, and then I'll show you my pond. The sweetest frogs live there. You will love them. Then you can join us at the celebration at the Seigneur's manor. Can you stay here for a while?"

"Yes. We can stay. Is it a holiday?" asked Emily as Marie milked her cow.

"It is like a holiday. It is the end of harvest, and later today, Papa will pay all his taxes to the Seigneur. We will soon eat lovely cakes and meet the Seigneur's children."

"That sounds like fun," said Matt.

"That sounds delicious. I love cakes," said Emily.

"Goodbye, Rosie," said Marie, patting her

cow on her head. Then she skipped out of the barn. "This way. Just watch where you step. Rosie has left dung everywhere."

This One's for You

Claire led them over Rosie's dung, over rocks, and through a leaf-covered path in the woods. "There's my pond," she called, running ahead.

Marie flopped down on the grass beside the pond. She pulled off her clogs and socks and tucked her skirt into her waistband. Then she dipped her feet into the pond.

Marie walked a little way into the pond. She bent over and picked up a small frog sunning itself on a rock. "It is so sweet," she said, patting the wiggly creature on the head.

Matt and Emily yanked off their clogs and socks. They dipped their feet into the pond.

As they sat back on the grass, Marie hurried over and thrust the frog into Matt's hands. "Hold it," she said.

The frog squirmed. "Yikes! It's slippery," said Matt.

"Of course it's slippery. It's a frog!" said Marie, giggling. "Is this the first frog you have ever held?"

Matt nodded.

"And you, too, Emily?"

"No. I've held a frog before but—"

Before Emily could finish her sentence, Marie picked up another frog and dropped it into Emily's lap. "This one's for you," she said.

The frog tried to jump out of Emily's lap.

"It wants to go back to its rock," said Emily.

She waded into the pond and slipped the frog back in. It dove quickly into the water.

"My frog wants to go home, too," said Matt. He waded into the pond and let his frog leap back in.

"I will show you more animals later. Are you hungry?" asked Marie. "I am so hungry, I could eat a whole loaf of bread by myself. Claire makes good bread. My father does not know how to bake, and I am not good at baking either."

Matt smiled. "I'm starved," he said.

"Me too," said Emily. "I love homemade bread."

The three children hurried along the path to the farmhouse.

Claire opened the door. "Come in, children," she greeted them.

Emily and Matt looked around the small

farmhouse. It had two rooms with a few simple pieces of wooden furniture. A table, four chairs, and two stools furnished the larger front room. Clothes hung on pegs on the wall. A big fireplace warmed the room. One large bed stood in the smaller room, with pegs on the wall for clothes.

There were also stairs leading to an upstairs space. "I sleep up there," Marie explained.

"Your father will join us soon, Marie," said Claire. "He said we should go ahead and eat before he comes. Then we will get ready to go to the celebration."

"Mmm. The bread smells delicious," said Matt.

"I made three loaves. I will take one to the Seigneur's manor," said Claire.

Claire turned to bring the bread and butter to the table. Just as Claire bent over the table,

Marie reached into her pocket. She pulled something wiggly out. Before the children could warn Claire, Marie dropped it on her stepmother's head.

Claire screamed. "Get it off!"

"It's just a little frog," said Marie, laughing. "It won't hurt you."

Claire pulled the frog out of her hair and handed it to Marie.

"I do not appreciate frogs in my hair, Marie," she said as Marie's father strode into the farmhouse.

5

Up the River

"What is all the screaming about?" he asked.

"I just gave Claire a little frog, and she screamed like a baby," said Marie.

"You put the frog in my hair," said Claire.

"It was just a joke. My mother would have laughed. She was not afraid of frogs. She was not afraid of anything."

Marie's father glared at his daughter. "You will not do this again. You will treat Claire with respect. She is your mother now. She has made us a good home."

"She is *not* my mother. She will never be my mother. I...I..." Marie glared at Claire.

"Enough, Marie," said her father. "Let us eat and get ready to go. Thank goodness I can pay off our taxes to the Seigneur; the harvest has been good this year."

Marie's father turned to Matt and Emily. "You will have to excuse my daughter's behaviour. Have you two just moved here?"

"They are my new friends, Emily and Matt," said Marie. "Can they please come with us to the Seigneur's celebration, Papa?"

"If they wish. I do not think the Seigneur will mind two more children. There will be other children at the celebration, and the Seigneur has three of his own. Perhaps you can all play together."

Marie clapped her hands. Then she turned to Emily and Matt. "We will have such fun."

"How do we get to the Seigneur's?" asked Matt.

"By canoe, of course," said Marie. "We have a large canoe. We will all fit."

Marie's father sat down and ate a chunk of bread. He turned to Claire. "This bread is wonderful, Claire."

Claire blushed. "Thank you, Pierre," she said.

Marie rolled her eyes at Emily and Matt. Then she tugged at her father's sleeve. "Papa, can I please sit in front of you in the canoe?"

"Well..." said her father, looking at Claire.

"It is fine with me," said Claire.

"You promise to behave properly at the manor, Marie?" said her father.

"Of course, Papa. I will be very good."

"Then let us clean up and go."

The children helped Claire tidy up the table

and cover the bread and butter. Claire wrapped the third loaf in a clean cloth.

Marie and Claire changed into fresh clothes and bonnets.

"This is my best dress," said Marie, spinning around to show her blue and white dress to Emily and Matt. "Do you like it?"

"Yes," said Emily. "It's pretty. I wish I had another dress to wear besides this one." Emily looked down at her dress. It was smeared with grass and wet at the bottom from the pond."

Soon everyone followed Pierre down a path through the woods to the river.

"There's our canoe!" said Marie. "I helped Papa build it out of birchbark. Isn't it beautiful?"

Pierre Dubois smiled. "I am glad we made it big enough so all of us could fit."

Pierre helped each person into the canoe.

Marie made sure she sat near her father's seat. Everyone else climbed carefully into the canoe. Pierre and Claire picked up paddles and pushed off from the riverbank.

"Wait until you see the manor house!" said Marie. "I have only visited once before, but it is beautiful! It is full of heavy carved-wood furniture that came all the way from France. There are beautiful dishes with little flowers on the bowls and plates. The wine glasses are so delicate I do not dare go near one. I would not want to break it."

"I am glad of that," said Pierre, laughing. "Marie likes to run around, and I worry that she might knock a glass or plate over. Then I would have to pay the Seigneur. I have no money for such things."

6

Lovely Cakes

Matt and Emily peered at the farms that hugged the shore as Pierre and Claire paddled upriver. They watched birds fly overhead and deer and rabbits scamper into the woods. A gentle breeze stirred the water.

They were so busy enjoying the scenery, they at first didn't see Marie pointing to a large stone house at the top of a hill.

"Emily and Matt, look. There is the manor house!" Marie said. "Oh, I hope they have those lovely cakes. The last time, I ate three."

"Marie!" said her father sternly. "You must only take one cake. We do not want the Seigneur and his family to think we are greedy."

"The cakes were small like this," said Marie. She cupped her hands together. Then she closed her eyes and smacked her lips. "They were so good. I could have eaten ten!"

Claire wrapped her shawl tightly around her shoulders. "It has suddenly turned cold, Pierre. Look at the darkening clouds."

"Do not worry. We will not stay long," said Pierre.

"We have to stay long enough to eat cakes and play with the Seigneur's children. I did not meet them last year. I hope they are here today," said Marie.

"We will need to keep an eye on the weather," said Pierre, paddling to shore. "Meanwhile, remember Marie—not too many cakes for you or your friends."

"Do not worry, Papa," said Marie. "We will be good. Right?" Marie smiled at Emily and Matt.

"We promise," said Emily.

"One cake is enough for me," said Matt.

"Here we are," said Pierre. He hopped out and dragged the canoe up on land. Two other canoes were pulled up on the shore close by.

One by one, the children and Claire stepped out of the canoe and onto a path, thick with yellow and red autumn leaves.

"It really *is* colder now," said Emily. She pulled her shawl around her shoulders too.

"And the sky's turning even darker than before," said Matt.

"Forget about the sky! Come on," said Marie, grabbing Emily's hand. "I will race you and Matt to the top of the hill. One. Two. Three. Go!"

The children raced up the leaf-covered hill to the top. Marie ran so fast, she was soon ahead of them.

"You win," said Emily as she and Matt reached the top, huffing and puffing.

"I am good at running. Papa says I am almost as fast as a fox," said Marie.

7

One Day

"One day I will live in a beautiful house like this!" said Marie, skipping toward the large house.

"Your house is cozy. I love the big fireplace," said Emily.

"But it is not grand," said Marie, sweeping her hand out toward the mansion. "And it does not have all these big windows to look out at everything."

Pierre knocked on the heavy carved wood door. A tall man in black knee-pants, a crisp white shirt, and a jacket with gold-coloured buttons opened the door.

Pierre introduced himself. "I am Pierre Dubois. This is my family and our two guests."

"The Seigneur expects you. Follow me," said the tall man.

They followed him into a large room filled with people. Candles set into silver candlesticks glittered everywhere. A white tablecloth covered a long table with carved wooden legs. The table was spread with bread, butter, preserves, and cakes of different sizes. Some were as small as cupcakes. The man who opened the door announced Pierre and his family.

A short man with a large protruding belly, black tights, a white ruffled shirt, and a red brocade jacket approached. "Welcome to my home. Come and enjoy some refreshments."

The room was filled with people. Many of the women wore long gowns decorated with lace and embroidery.

Marie hurried toward the table, but Pierre caught her arm. "Remember, you promised to behave like a proper young lady."

"I will, Father."

Marie, Emily, and Matt each picked up a small cake and took a bite.

"It is as delicious as I remembered," said Marie.

"It's awesome!" said Matt, smacking his lips. He took a second piece of a white cake filled with raisins and nuts.

"I taste maple syrup in this one," said Emily. "Mmm. I love maple syrup."

"Let us talk to the Seigneur's children. There they are at the other end of the table," said Marie.

The three friends approached the Seigneur's children. The two girls were dressed in lacy blue and pink gowns. They had pink velvet ribbons in their hair.

The older girl looked about eleven, and the younger about eight. The boy was dressed like his father, the Seigneur. He looked about twelve.

"I am Marie Dubois, and these are my friends, Emily and Matt."

The boy stared at Marie, Emily, and Matt's outfits. "You are habitants' children," he said. "You work my father's land." He sniffed at them as if they smelled bad.

"Marie is Pierre Dubois' daughter, and we're visitors," said Emily.

The boy raised his eyebrows. "I am Robert, and these are my sisters, Madeleine and Anne."

The two girls giggled. They stared at Marie and Emily, and at Matt's clothes, too.

"Is it true that habitants live in dark, dirty houses with their cows?" asked Madeleine, the older of the girls.

"I...I..." Marie hesitated. She looked stunned, as if she'd been punched in the stomach.

"Marie does not live with the cows or any other animals," said Matt.

"And her house is cozy and warm," said Emily.

Robert and Madeleine rolled their eyes at each other. Anne said nothing. She looked down at the floor.

"Well, I can only tell you what I heard, and the person who told me never makes things up," said Madeleine. "Come, Anne, we must speak to Mama."

"I do not want to speak to Mama now. I want to stay here," said Anne.

Madeleine grabbed her little sister's hand. "We must speak to Mama *now*," she insisted.

"Goodbye," Anne said to Marie, Emily, and Matt, as her sister hurried her away.

8

How Could They?

"How could they say that? How could they treat us like that?" cried Marie. Tears spilled from her eyes.

"They are so mean! I...I..." she sputtered. Then she turned and ran out of the dining room.

"Wait!" called Matt, but Marie was gone.

"Poor Marie. Those kids were horrid to her," said Emily. "Well, except for Anne."

"Where do you think she went?" asked Matt.

"I don't know. Let's see if she's in the hall."

Matt and Emily hurried into the hall. Robert, Madeleine, and Anne were staring out through one of the windows at the back of the house.

"What a stupid habitant," said Robert.

"My friend says that habitants know nothing about proper behaviour. And did you see their miserable clothes?" said Madeleine. "They look like beggars."

"I liked Marie and her friends," said Anne.

Robert waved his hand at his little sister. "What do you know? You are too little."

Emily marched over to the three children. "And you're so mean. You think you're special because you're rich and wear fancy clothes with lace and velvet. Well, you're—"

"Not!" Matt chimed in. "Marie and her family are nice."

"How dare you speak to us like that!" screeched Madeleine. "Go back to your filthy farmhouse and dirty friends. Come, Robert. And you, too, Anne."

"I don't want to," said Anne. She scrunched up her nose and glared at her sister.

"Come," Robert ordered her, "or I will tell Papa you were naughty."

Robert grabbed Anne's hand and yanked her away. Anne glanced back at Emily and Matt as she left.

"Can you imagine being their sister?" said Emily.

"Poor Anne, and poor Marie. Where did she go, anyway?"

Matt and Emily looked out the hall window.

"Look! There she is!" said Matt. "She's heading for the woods."

"And the wind is blowing hard now."

"Do you think she knows her way around here? We're pretty far from her farmhouse," said Matt.

"Come on. We have to stop her!"

Emily and Matt raced to the front door.

"If we run, maybe we can reach her before she gets lost in those woods," said Matt.

"We'd better find her before Pierre and Claire decide to go home."

"It's starting to snow!" said Matt as they slipped out the door. They rushed down the front steps of the manor.

Emily peered ahead. "Oh no! I don't see her anymore. She was running pretty fast. What if we can't find her in time?"

"We have to find her," said Matt. "Brr. It's getting colder now." Matt pulled his cap lower and his jacket tighter. "And the snow is coming down harder."

"We'd better not get lost," said Emily as they approached the woods.

Matt pulled off his wool scarf. He yanked at a loose thread, and it began to unravel. He bit into a strand and wrapped it around a tree. "This will help us find our way out."

9

Footsteps

Matt and Emily ventured into the thick woods.

"Marie! Where are you?" called Emily.

"We're here!" called Matt.

"And we're your friends!" said Emily.

Matt tied a new piece of red wool around another tree. Matt and Emily listened for footsteps, but all they could hear was the rustle of the wind.

Matt pulled out his recorder and spoke into it. "We are in New France, in deep, dark woods. We're looking for our friend, Marie, but we don't know where she is. Will we find her? Stay tuned."

"I'm freezing," said Emily, shivering.

Matt snapped his recorder off. "Me too." He clapped his hands together.

"My jacket isn't warm enough. We can't stay out here much longer, or we're going to turn into icicles."

"But we have to find Marie," said Matt.

"Maybe she went back, and we just didn't see her."

"Let's walk a little farther into the woods and then turn back. We'll need to get help right away if she's not back at the manor."

Matt and Emily walked deeper into the woods, but there was still no sign of Marie.

"Okay. Let's turn back now," said Matt.

"How do we get out of here?"

Matt groaned. "Oh, no! I was so busy looking for Marie, I forgot to tie any more wool on the trees."

"What now?" said Emily. "The woods look the same from every direction."

Matt gulped. "Let's try that way. See, there are some of our footprints in the snow." He pointed to the left.

They walked to the left, but there was no sign of Marie or the wool on the trees.

"There are no more footprints. They're covered in fresh snow already. Maybe we should we go right," said Emily.

"I don't know," said Matt. "I wish I'd remembered to tie the wool so this wouldn't have happened."

"It's not your fault. I forgot about it, too. But what are we going to do? We're lost! And it's getting colder and snowier."

Matt grabbed Emily's arm. "Don't move. I hear footsteps."

Matt and Emily stopped walking and listened.

"I hear it, too. Do you think it's a person or an animal?" asked Emily.

"I don't know. Let's call out."

"Hello! Hello? Who's there?" they called.

No one answered.

Matt shrugged. "All I hear is the wind."

"Wait! I hear footsteps again. The sound is coming closer. Hello! Help! Who's out there?" called Emily.

"Whooo are youuu?" came a voice.

"There *is* someone out there! But who and where? Keep calling!" said Matt.

Matt and Emily yelled at the top of their lungs. "Hello! This way! Follow our voices!"

For a minute there was no answer, and then they heard a voice. "I hear you! Keep calling. I will come!"

"There *is* someone," said Emily.

"This way! We're here!" Matt and Emily shouted until they were hoarse.

"I see you!" cried the voice. "I'm coming!"

10

Lost and Found

It was a man, and he was holding something—or someone—in his arms. They could see him like a shadow through the trees.

"Who are you?" he called.

"I'm Matt, and this is Emily. We're lost, and we're looking for our friend, Marie Dubois."

"I have found her," said the man. He came closer. Now they could see him! He was dressed in thick brown pants, a heavy, worn jacket, and high boots. He was carrying a girl in his arms.

"Oh, no! Sh-she's not..." stammered Emily.

"I am not dead," said the girl in a weak, tired voice.

"Marie!" called Emily and Matt. They rushed toward the man and the girl.

"It *is* you!" said Emily. "We're so glad to see you."

"And I am so glad to be found. I fell," whimpered Marie. "Jacques found me just in time."

"I am a *coureur de bois*," Jacques explained. "I was on my way home after two months trapping beavers. I found your friend caught in a deer snare. I fear she's hurt her leg."

"Her family is visiting the manor, but we don't know how to get there from here. We're lost," said Matt.

"I know the manor well, and I know these woods. Follow me," said Jacques.

Emily and Matt followed Jacques through the woods. The snow had slowed down, but the wind blew snow from the trees and bushes into their faces.

"What is this?" asked Jacques as they passed a tree where Matt had left a piece of red wool.

"I put it there to help us find our way out," said Matt.

Jacques smiled. "It was a good plan, but you should have wrapped more pieces of wool on more trees."

Matt grinned. "I know," he said.

"There's the manor!" called Emily. The group strode quickly toward the house.

"There's Pierre and Claire!" said Matt. Marie's father and stepmother were running toward them from the house.

"Marie!" cried Claire, when she reached her stepdaughter. "We were so worried. We feared the worst."

Claire stroked Marie's hair.

"I am fine, Claire. Really I am. My leg hurts, but that is all."

"Thank goodness you have all been found," said Pierre. "I must tell the Seigneur that you are safe. He sent two men out to look for you. Why did you go to the woods? You do not know these woods. You must never do such a thing again."

"Marie ran away because Robert and Madeleine were mean to her. They said terrible things to her," said Emily. "We ran out to find her, but we got lost."

"We know about the children's cruel words to Marie," said Claire as they walked to the manor. "Anne told her father what her brother and sister said. The Seigneur is angry with his two older children, and they are angry their sister told their father what happened."

"I hope Robert and Madeleine do not make Anne's life miserable," said Marie. "I like Anne. She is kind."

"They will not make my little Anne unhappy," said the Seigneur, approaching. "She was right to tell me what happened. My children were wrong to treat our guests in such a disrespectful manner. You have my apologies. I am happy you have all been found safely."

"Thank you," said Marie. "Now, please, Papa, can we go home?"

11

Home

They bundled Marie up in a blanket and set her in Claire's arms in the canoe. Matt sat near Pierre, and Emily sat in the back.

"I wish you a safe journey home," said the Seigneur as Pierre pushed off from the riverbank. "I hope Marie's leg will heal quickly."

Jacques bid them goodbye and wished them well. "It is not far to my home," he told them. "It will be good to see my wife and son after so long."

Snow began to fall harder again as they

passed the manor and headed down the river.
The river was choppy now, and the canoe rose
and fell in the churning waves.

"We must get home soon," said Pierre,
paddling quickly. Matt helped paddle, too.

"How is the pain, Marie?" asked Claire.

"My leg hurts," said Marie. "Do you think it
is broken?"

"No. I do not think so. I think you have just
sprained it badly, but it will heal."

"My face feels hot," said Marie.

Claire touched her face. "I think you may be
feverish now, Marie."

Marie closed her eyes and leaned against
Claire. Emily looked at Matt. She knew he was
thinking the same thing she was. Marie was
letting Claire take care of her at last.

"I am so tired, so hot, and so wet," murmured
Marie.

"We will be home soon, and then I will give you some good hot soup. You will be better in no time, Marie."

"Thank you, Claire," said Marie.

Claire reached out and held Marie's hand. Marie smiled.

The waves rose higher as the snow came down stronger and harder. No one spoke as Pierre and Matt dipped their paddles in and out of the icy water.

Emily glanced up. The sky was beginning to get darker. It would soon be night. When would they make it back to the farmhouse? They were all shivering and Marie was groaning in pain. She looked really sick now.

Claire whispered comforting words to Marie, but the expression on Claire's face told Emily and Matt that she was worried about her step-daughter, too.

"There's the farmhouse!" called Matt. "We're almost back!"

Pierre looked up. "Thank goodness," he said. "It will be dark any moment now. We must get Marie home. We need to all get inside and light a fire. It will be a cold night, and you children must stay. I hope your family will not worry."

"They won't," said Matt.

"I am sure they realize that you could not go out on such a terrible night," said Pierre as they neared the riverbank beside the farmhouse. Pierre jumped out of the canoe. He tied it to a large log beside the river. Then he lifted Marie out and carried her as everyone followed him to the farmhouse.

12

Good Soup

Pierre put Marie to bed as Claire built a fire in the fireplace. "I made soup earlier. I will warm it up for everyone," she said. She placed a large black pot over a hook above the fire.

Soon a wonderful smell of onions and peas filled the farmhouse. When the soup was hot, Claire gave Marie a steaming bowl. But Marie could only eat a few mouthfuls. She waved the soup away. "I am so tired," she whispered. "Please sit beside me, Claire, till I fall asleep."

"Of course I will," said Claire.

"You must eat, children," Pierre coaxed Emily and Matt. He brought them each a hot bowl of soup.

Matt dipped his spoon in and sipped. "This is the best pea soup I've ever tasted," he said.

"I usually hate pea soup," said Emily, "but this is delicious! I wish I could give my mom your recipe."

"I would be happy to tell your mama how to make the soup," said Claire. "I would like to meet her one day."

"She would like you a lot," said Emily.

"Would you tell me how to make it so I can tell her as soon as I get home?"

As they sat by the fire and savoured their soup with bread and butter, Claire told Emily how she made her soup.

"I am weary," said Pierre. "You must all be weary, too. Let us get some sleep."

"I hope Marie will be better tomorrow," said Emily.

"I hope so, too," said Pierre, sighing. He glanced up at the attic where his daughter slept.

Pierre and Claire spread blankets on the floor for Emily and Matt, and everyone went to bed.

"This floor feels like a rock, but I'm so tired I could fall asleep standing up," Emily whispered to Matt.

Matt didn't answer. He was already asleep.

Before Emily knew it, it was morning. Sun lit up the one small window in the front room.

"Matt, it's morning. Get up. We'd better check on the sled. We almost forgot about it!"

"Soon," said Matt turning over.

"Come on. Now."

"Okay," grunted Matt. He stood up.

Claire was up already, lighting a fire.

"How's Marie?" asked Matt.

"Her fever broke late last night," said Claire, smiling. "I know she will be fine. We will all be fine now."

Emily and Matt smiled at each other. They knew what Claire meant. Claire, Pierre, and Marie would really be a family now.

"We have to go outside and check on our sled," said Emily.

"We might have to go home right away, too," said Matt.

"Please say goodbye to Marie and Pierre from us," Emily said.

"I will," said Claire. "I hope we see you soon again."

Emily and Matt waved goodbye as they opened the door.

The air was crisp and cold, but the snow had stopped. The ground was blanketed with white.

They scurried to the spot where they'd left the sled. It poked out through the snow.

They brushed the snow off the top. As soon as they did, shimmery gold words began to form.

"It's time to go home," said Matt. "Look what it says!"

You were lost in the snow,
But soon you were found.
Now sit on the sled,
For home you are bound.

Emily and Matt hopped on the sled. Emily rubbed the maple leaf three times. The sled rose over the woods, over Marie's farmhouse, over the river, and into the fluffy white cloud.

Soon they were back in the tower room.

"Oops! I forget to sketch anything on this adventure. I don't want to forget what Marie and her family looked like," said Emily as she slid off the sled.

She pulled her sketchbook out of her pocket and sat cross-legged on the floor. She sketched Marie dropping a frog on Claire's head.

"Remember this?" she asked Matt.

"Of course. Do you remember Claire's pea soup recipe?"

"Of course. You take a handful of pebbles, a pocketful of fall leaves, some peas, and mush them all together. Then you cook them over a low fire for an hour."

"You do not," said Matt. "I bet you don't remember what Claire told you."

"I do, too, and I'm going to tell my mom how to make it today. You can have some if you come over after school tomorrow. I might even bring some for show-off Sarah at school. I'll tell her the king's daughter gave me the recipe."

"She won't know what you're talking about," said Matt.

Emily laughed. "I know!"

MORE ABOUT...

After their adventure, Emily and Matt wanted to know more about New France and the king's daughters (filles du roi). Turn the page for their favourite facts.

Emily's Top Ten Facts

1. In the mid 1600s, Quebec seigneurs and their families copied fancy French fashions. They wore clothes made out of silk, velvet, and lace.

2. The habitants made their clothes out of linen, hemp, or wool. They lined their clothes with fur or leather to make them warmer.

3. Habitant families grew almost all their own food. Peas and corn were the most popular vegetables.

And they made awesome pea soup from all those peas —M.

4. Habitant families usually made all their own clothes, curtains, rugs, towels, soap, furniture, and candles.

5. Unlike the coureurs du bois, the habitants didn't have to do any military duty.

6. The habitants celebrated Christmas, Easter, and November eleventh, the day they paid their taxes. They welcomed spring with May Day celebrations.

7. The habitants worked hard from the time they woke up in the morning to the time they went to bed.

8. This is how you milk a cow: first, wash and dry the udder. Then pinch the top of a teat with your thumb and forefinger. Next, use your other fingers like you were squeezing water out of a hose.

Want to try milking a cow again, Em? —M.

9. The coureurs du bois often lived with the First Peoples while they traded with them. They usually trapped beaver, because their fur was popular and they could make good money selling their pelts.

10. In 1696, King Louis XIV refused to let the coureurs du bois trade any more. He said they were neglecting their families, their land, and the colony of Quebec.

Matt's Top Ten Facts

1. In the mid 1600s, one in four people lived in New France's towns. The other three-quarters lived on farms.

2. In 1700, Quebec was the largest town in New France and had a population of about 2,000 people. It was also the colony's main port.

3. Montreal, founded in 1642, soon became the second-largest city in New France because of its busy fur trade.

4. Rich people, the Church, and government officers were in the upper part of Quebec City. Artisans (like carpenters and toolmakers) and merchants had businesses in the lower part of the city.

5. By the middle of the 1700s, most of the houses in New France were made of stone, because fires destroyed homes made of wood.

6. New France towns weren't very clean. The narrow streets were full of garbage. When it grew hot, the streets became dusty; and when it rained, they were muddy.

Phew! I'm glad we weren't there in the summer. -E.

7. Most habitants lived on long narrow lots, and they built their homes near the river.

8. New France settlers often travelled by boat along the rivers. The First Peoples taught the habitants how to construct good canoes.

9. The usual drinks in New France were water, spruce beer, or red wine mixed with water.

Nine brothers and sisters! Yikes! -E.

10. Many New France families were big. Some families had more than ten children!

So You Want to Know...
FROM AUTHOR FRIEDA WISHINSKY

When I was writing this book, my friends wanted to know more about the filles du roi and New France. I told them that *Lost in the Snow is* based on historical facts, but all the characters are made up. Here are some other questions I answered.

Who discovered New France?

Jacques Cartier was the first to explore the St. Lawrence River region in 1534. He landed in the Gaspé Peninsula and claimed it for France. The following year, he landed in what is now Quebec City. He was excited because he thought he'd found gold in the area; but to his disappointment, he had not. The French were so discouraged about the difficulties of exploring the region and the absence of gold that they didn't return for sixty-six years.

How was New France settled?

In the early 1600s, the king saw that the fur trade in the New World could make a lot of money for France. But he knew they needed to claim the land for France by establishing people in settlements, or colonies, in the Saint Lawrence River Valley. In 1608, the explorer Samuel Champlain traded with the local Algonquin Nation. He knew the settlers needed the help of the Native people to survive the harsh winters, and to learn how to hunt and build homes. It took many years, but by the late 1600s (after Champlain's death), New France was firmly established.

How did the filles du roi (the King's Daughters) program start?

In the mid 1600s, New France had six men to every woman settler. King Louis XIV of France wanted the colony to grow but knew it would be hard with so few families. King Louis and his advisors came up with an unusual plan. They encouraged unmarried women to travel to New France and marry settlers. Many of these women were poor or orphaned, and many came from the countryside. The king offered the women money to make the long, difficult journey across the Atlantic, and even more if they married settlers.

How much did it cost the king to send each woman to New France?

It cost the equivalent of about $1,500 in today's money. Each woman was also given practical items such as a bonnet, handkerchiefs, stockings, gloves, ribbons, shoelaces, white thread, needles, pins, a comb, a pair of scissors, and two knives. When she arrived in New France, she also received clothing and other supplies to help her in her new life.

How long did the filles du roi program last?

The program was a great success. Many young women came to New France to marry settlers. By 1673, ten years after the program started, many families had been established. There was therefore no need to send any more women over to New France and the program ended.

What was the seigniorial system of farming in New France?

To encourage the settlement of New France, King Louis offered free land to nobles, priests and other religious leaders, and other important people (including women). These new landowners were called seigneurs. In exchange for the land, they promised the king that they would divide their land into smaller sections, which would be farmed by other settlers, called habitants. The habitants did not own the land, but they could live on the land by paying taxes to the seigneur.

When and how did New France come under English rule?

The French and the English in North America often fought over land. During the Seven Years War between England and France, the English in the New World gradually took over control of New France. Yet, even without much help from France, the French settlers thrived in Quebec and the French colony survived for 150 years.

Coming next in the
Canadian Flyer Adventures Series...

Canadian Flyer Adventures
#11

Far from
Home

Matt and Emily help refugee children
during the Second World War.

Visit
www.mapletreepress.com/canadianflyeradventures
for a sneak peek at the latest book in the series.

The *Canadian Flyer* Adventures Series

#1 Beware, Pirates! **#2 Danger, Dinosaurs!** **#3 Crazy for Gold**

#4 Yikes, Vikings! **#5 Flying High!** **#6 Pioneer Kids** **#7 Hurry, Freedom**

#8 A Whale Tale   **#9 All Aboard!**   **#10 Lost in the Snow**

Upcoming Book

Look out for the next book that will take Emily and Matt on a new adventure:

#11 Far from Home

And more to come!

More Praise for the Series

"[Emily and Matt] learn more than they ever could have from a history textbook. Every book in this new series promises to shed light on a different chapter of Canadian history."
~ *MONTREAL GAZETTE*

"Readers are in for a great adventure."
~ *EDMONTON'S CHILD*

"This series makes Canadian history fun, exciting and accessible."
~ *CHRONICLE HERALD (HALIFAX)*

"[An] enthralling series for junior-school readers."
~ *HAMILTON SPECTATOR*

"...highly entertaining, very educational but not too challenging. A terrific new series."
~ *RESOURCE LINKS*

"This wonderful new Canadian historical adventure series combines magic and history to whisk young readers away on adventure...A fun way to learn about Canada's past."
~ *BC PARENT*

"Highly recommended."
~ *CM: CANADIAN REVIEW OF MATERIALS*

Teacher Resource Guides now available online.
Please visit our website at
www.mapletreepress.com/canadianflyeradventures
to download tips and ideas for
using the series in the classroom.

About the Author

Frieda Wishinsky, a former teacher, is an award-winning picture- and chapter-book author, who has written many beloved and bestselling books for children. Frieda enjoys using humour and history in her work, while exploring new ways to tell a story. Her books have earned much critical praise, including a nomination for a Governor General's Award in 1999. In addition to the books in the *Canadian Flyer Adventures* series, Frieda has published *What's the Matter with Albert?*, *A Quest in Time*, and *Manya's Dream* with Maple Tree Press. Frieda lives in Toronto.

About the Illustrator

Leanne Franson has drawn as long as she can remember, and even before! She drew in her school notebooks, on scrap paper, on the sidewalk. And she read and read, especially stories that took place in the past, or had children who travelled to other and distant worlds. Leanne has lent her pencil and brush to over 80 books, and is happy to be accompanying Matt and Emily back into history in the *Canadian Flyer Adventures* series. Leanne works at home in Montreal, where she lives with her son Benjamin Taotao, her Saint Bernard, Gretchen, and two cats.